On Linden Square

Words and Pictures by
Kate Sullivan

It was the first day of winter vacation and Stella Mae Culpepper was bored to tears. She watched the sun sink slowly behind the apartment building across the street.

Fernando, her upstairs neighbor, liked to play video games and sing karaoke. She could hear him singing. Off-key.

Her downstairs neighbor, Miss Arpeggio, was rather large and played *Moonlight Sonata* on the piano during lightning storms.

From her tall bay windows on the second floor, Stella Mae could see the whole neighborhood.

She watched the tiny lady who talked to herself in a high squeaky voice as she clicked down the street every afternoon. Stella Mae called her Mouse Lady, but never to her face.

She saw the old man in the porkpie hat who pedaled by on his rickety bicycle to collect the empty bottles out of the trash.

The neighbors' lights began to come on,

one

by

one.

Mr. Rubenstein lived in the house next door to Stella Mae's. He read lots of books and had two kitty cats, Pianissimo and Fortissimo.

Above him lived Mr. and Mrs. Chatterjee who didn't talk much. They wore Mexican hats and had a Chihuahua named Mahjong.

In the apartment building across the street, the two kids on the top floor had bunk beds and pillow fights.

On the floor below, a guy with a pencil mustache practiced the slide trombone.

The couple on the ground floor wore fancy clothes and went out in taxicabs.

They all lived on Linden Square.

Miss Arpeggio never said hello to Bottle Man.

Taxicab Couple never waved to Mr. and Mrs. Chatterjee.

Trombone Guy and Mouse Lady never crossed paths.

Pillow Fight Kids ran away
whenever Fernando sang

and Stella Mae never said hello to any of
them because they never said hello to her.

But that night as the sky grew darker, in the glow of the streetlights, she could see . . .

snow!

Snow began to cover the street and sidewalk, blowing a wintry frosting over the neighborhood. It snowed all night, all the next day, and into the next night.

When Stella Mae awoke the next morning, everything was white.

The cars looked like elephants. The telephone lines sagged like lazy white snakes. The trees sparkled with tangles of snowy spider webs. And every spike on the park fence sported a pointy snowcap.

Stella Mae pulled on her coat and her boots, ran across the street to the park, and squeezed through the gate. The snow was practically up to her armpits.

"Holy moly!" she whispered.

She made a little snowball and rolled it in the sticky snow. "This will be the tail," she thought.

The Pillow Fight Kids came outside to throw snowballs instead of pillows.

"Want to help?" called Stella Mae from the park.

Higher and higher went the mound of snow.

Trombone Guy stopped *wah-wah*ing and came outside, dragging a shovel. He came over to the park and started to make a huge head with bulging cheeks like Dizzy Gillespie.

One by one the neighbors came out to see what was going on.

Fernando pressed pause on his video game and set to work carving horns on top of the head.

Taxicab Couple pulled on their dressy boots and started sculpting dancing feet and a fancy crown.

Mr. and Mrs. Chatterjee came outside to let Mahjong make some yellow snow.
They stopped to watch the neighbors. "What are you making?" they asked.

"Hmmm . . . it's . . . a ballerina?" suggested Taxicab Couple.

"It's Ferdinand the Bull?" offered Fernando.

"No, it's a scatty-wah, scatty-wah jazzman!" sang Trombone Guy.

"It looks like Babar, the French elephant," said Miss Arpeggio.

"Maybe it is Ganesh, the very lucky Indian elephant-man who rides on a mouse!" Mrs. Chatterjee chirped.

Mouse Lady squeaked by and thought it should have whiskers.

"No, I think it's that mean old witch, Baba Yaga," Mr. Rubenstein said.

"Baba Yaga! Baba Yaga!" chanted the Pillow Fight Kids. (They just liked the sound of it.)

Bottle Man put on his brakes to think.
"Very feng shui. Let's just call it . . ."

"Ferdinand Ganesh,
the Jazzy Dancing
Baba Feng Shui
Elephant-Mouse!"
shouted Stella Mae triumphantly.

The neighbors all looked at one another. Then they looked at their sculpture.

"Yes, that's what it is! Ferdinand Ganesh, the Jazzy Dancing Baba Feng Shui Elephant-Mouse!" they all agreed.

The neighbors stayed outside all day. Mr. Rubenstein brought out a tray of leftover latkes and performed a magic trick with his thumbs.

Fernando mulled some cider for everyone and sang "Ay, ay, ay, ay, Canta y no llores . . ."

The Chatterjees ran inside to get their special curry-flavored tacos while Miss Arpeggio and Trombone Guy babbled excitedly about playing duets.

In the meantime, Bottle Man wound a slip-slidy bicycle path through the park and decorated it with no-deposit bottles.

As dusk fell, the Chatterjees lit some candles, Trombone Guy played a tango, and everyone danced by the candlelight.

The clouds pressed lower and the streetlights came on.

One by one, the neighbors laughed, blew out their candles, and said goodnight.

Then Stella Mae Culpepper went home,
warmed her toes by the radiator,

and dreamed about
Ferdinand Ganesh,
    the Jazzy Dancing Baba Feng Shui Elephant-Mouse,

and what might happen on the next day of winter vacation.

Glossary

You will find many interesting words in *On Linden Square*. Some are related to musical concepts; others are literary or cultural references. In order of the word's appearance in the book, you will find definitions below.

Karaoke: a recording that plays a song with all the instruments except the voice. When you sing karaoke, it's your job to sing the song that's missing.

Off-key: When somebody sings off-key, their voice is just a bit higher or lower than it's supposed to be. The song sounds a little funny—not quite right.

Arpeggio: In music, whenever you play three or more notes at the same time, it's called a chord. An arpeggio is like a broken chord—instead of playing the notes together, you play the notes of the chord one at a time in a row, either up or down.

Moonlight Sonata: Ludwig van Beethoven was a famous German composer (1770–1827) who wrote many beautiful musical pieces. *Moonlight Sonata* is one of his most famous sonatas. It's full of arpeggios!

Pianissimo: In music, Italian words are used to tell a musician how to play. *Piano* is Italian for softly. *Pianissimo* means VERY softly!

Fortissimo: Italian for very loud.

Mahjong: an ancient Chinese game played with tiles decorated with Chinese characters or symbols.

Slide trombone: A musical instrument in the brass family, the trombone is played by blowing into a mouthpiece while you slide a movable section in and out to change the pitch.

Dizzy Gillespie: a great American jazz trumpeter, famous for puffing his cheeks full of air while he played.

Ferdinand the Bull: *The Story of Ferdinand* is about a peace-loving bull who would rather smell flowers than fight in bullfights.

Scatty-wah, scatty-wah jazzman: Jazz music is full of improvisation—music that is made up on the spot—so the music is full of surprises! If you can't remember the words or the tune, you make something up that will fit right in. The best players are really good at making stuff up—scatty-wah, scatty-wah, skibbety-scooba-dooba, doo-wah, ska-dootin'dooby-doo-wah!

Babar: a very famous French elephant who first appeared in the children's book, *Histoire de Babar (The Story of Babar)*.

Ganesh: a much-loved god in the Hindu religion in India. Ganesh has the head of an elephant, a big belly, and four arms! He loves all arts and music and science. He is a very happy god!

Baba Yaga: In Russian folklore, Baba Yaga is the supernatural being (ghost) who looks like a ferocious old woman.

Feng shui: a Chinese system to improve your life by paying attention to the five elements of wood, fire, earth, metal, and water. According to feng shui practice, in order to be happy, we need to balance the energy of these five elements.

Ay ay ay ay Canta y no llores: the chorus of a famous Mexican song, "Cielito Lindo." In the song, a man is singing to his girlfriend. He tells her to sing (*canta*) and not to cry (*no llores*), because singing makes you happy!

Tango: a dance from South America. The couple holds each other very close while they move in many different steps, some very fast, some very slow, depending on how the music makes them feel.

To my dear Bill, who lights the path every day.

For neighbors, with all their quirks and quips,
triumphs and squabbles, shortcomings and "longcomings."

To Brookline, Massachusetts,
whose elegant parks grace the lives of all who live there.

And to my aunt Joan, who at 87
still plays Beethoven during lightning storms.

–Kate

Sleeping Bear Press™

315 E. Eisenhower Parkway, Ste. 200
Ann Arbor, MI 48108
www.sleepingbearpress.com

Printed and bound in the United States.

10 9 8 7 6 5 4 3 2 1

Library of Congress Cataloging-in-Publication Data

Sullivan, Kate (Kate M.), 1950- author, illustrator.
On Linden Square / by Kate Sullivan.
pages cm
Summary: After a heavy snowfall, Stella Mae Culpepper goes to the park
and starts sculpting, and soon all of her neighbors, normally detached and
indifferent, are working together to build a fantastic snow creature.
ISBN 978-1-58536-832-7
[1. Neighborhood—Fiction. 2. Snow sculpture—Fiction. 3. Snow—Fiction.
4. Youths' writings.] I. Title.
PZ.S9524On 2013
[E]—dc23
2013004097